A Very Full
Morning

To Judy Sue, who taught me a lot of things,
including how to smile.

The text of this book is set in Optima.
The illustrations are acrylic and colored pencils on paper.

Library of Congress Cataloging-in-Publication Data

Montanari, Eva, 1977-
A very full morning / written and illustrated by Eva Montanari.
p. cm.
Summary: When Little Tooth goes to her first day of school, she learns that she is not the only rabbit who is anxious.
ISBN 0-618-56318-0 (hardcover)
[1. First day of school—Fiction. 2. Schools—Fiction. 3. Rabbits—Fiction.] I. Title.
PZ7.M76344
[Ver 2006]
[E]—dc22
2005033262

ISBN-13: 978-0618-56318-0

Manufactured in China
SCP 10 9 8 7 6 5 4 3 2 1

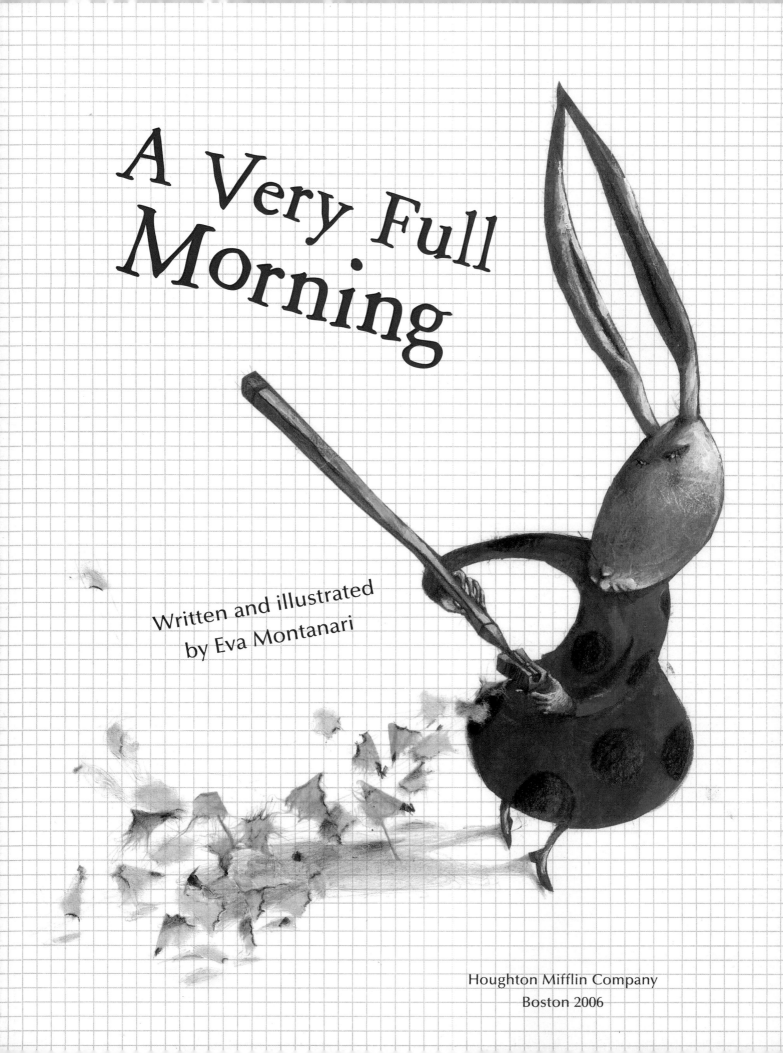

A Very Full Morning

Written and illustrated
by Eva Montanari

Houghton Mifflin Company

Boston 2006

Tonight Little Tooth tries to go to bed early.

Tomorrow morning she has to go to a very special place.

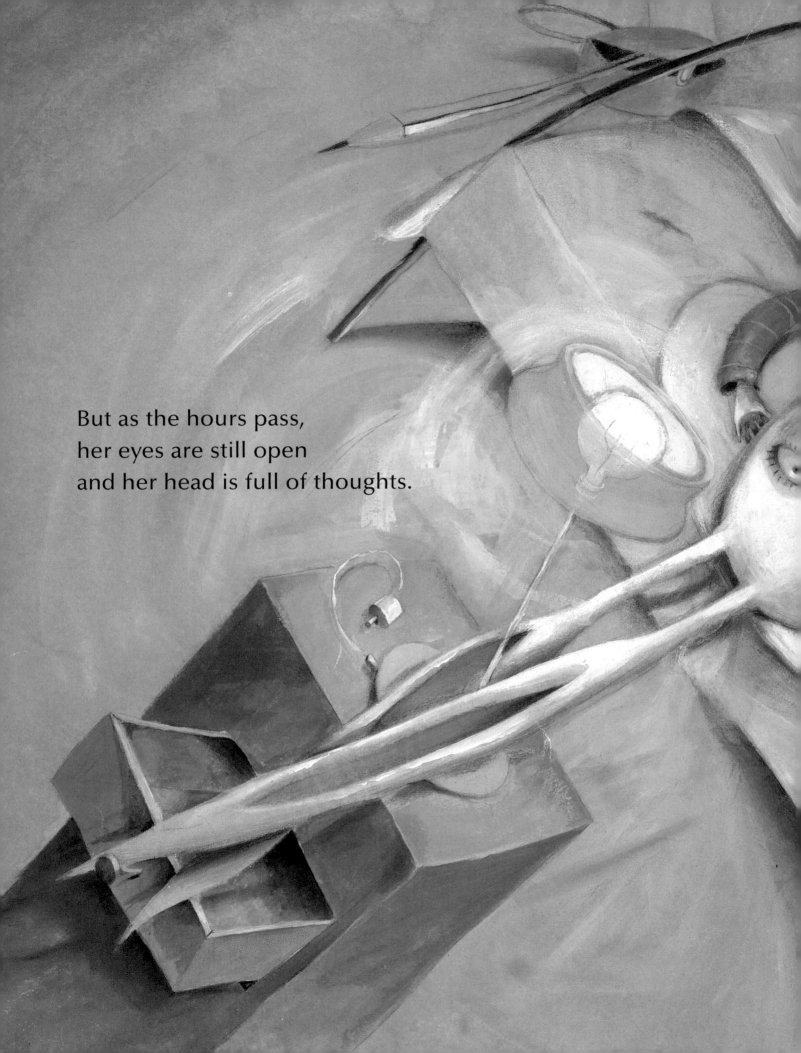

But as the hours pass,
her eyes are still open
and her head is full of thoughts.

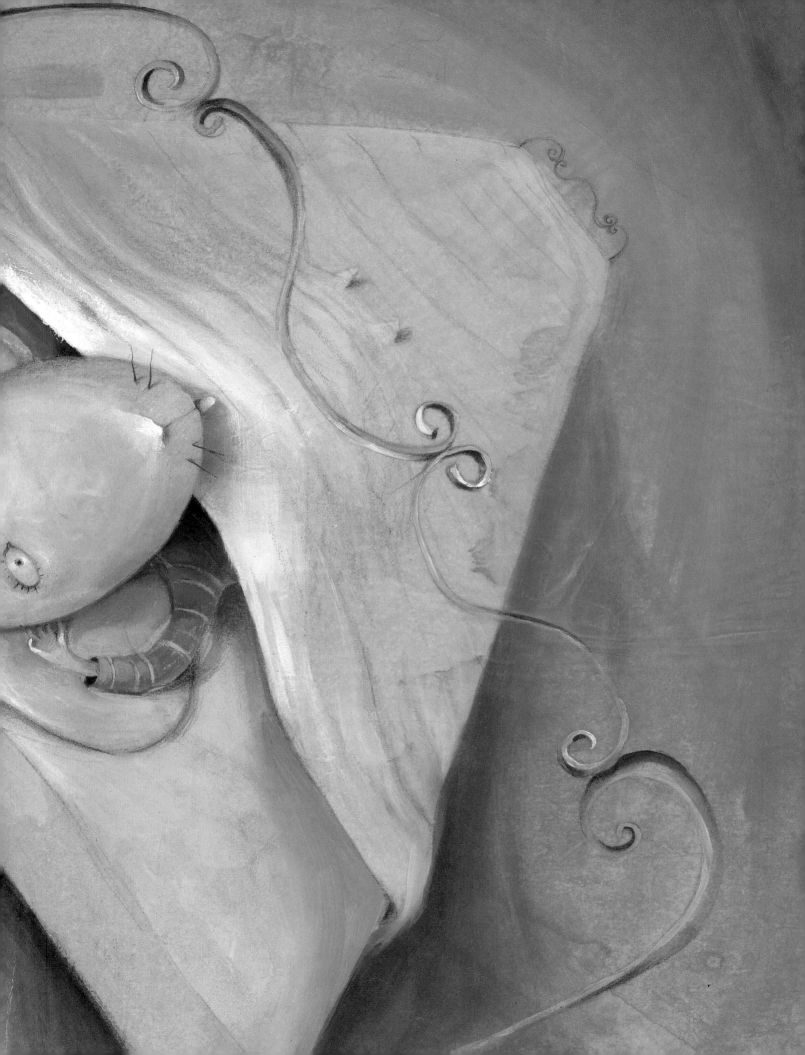

Finally the special morning arrives.

Little Tooth chooses a dress from her closet full of clothes, and she has a very special breakfast.

She sets off and comes to a gate full of bars.

She walks along a path full of stones.

She comes to a yard full of bags.

She follows the bags to a corridor full of doors.

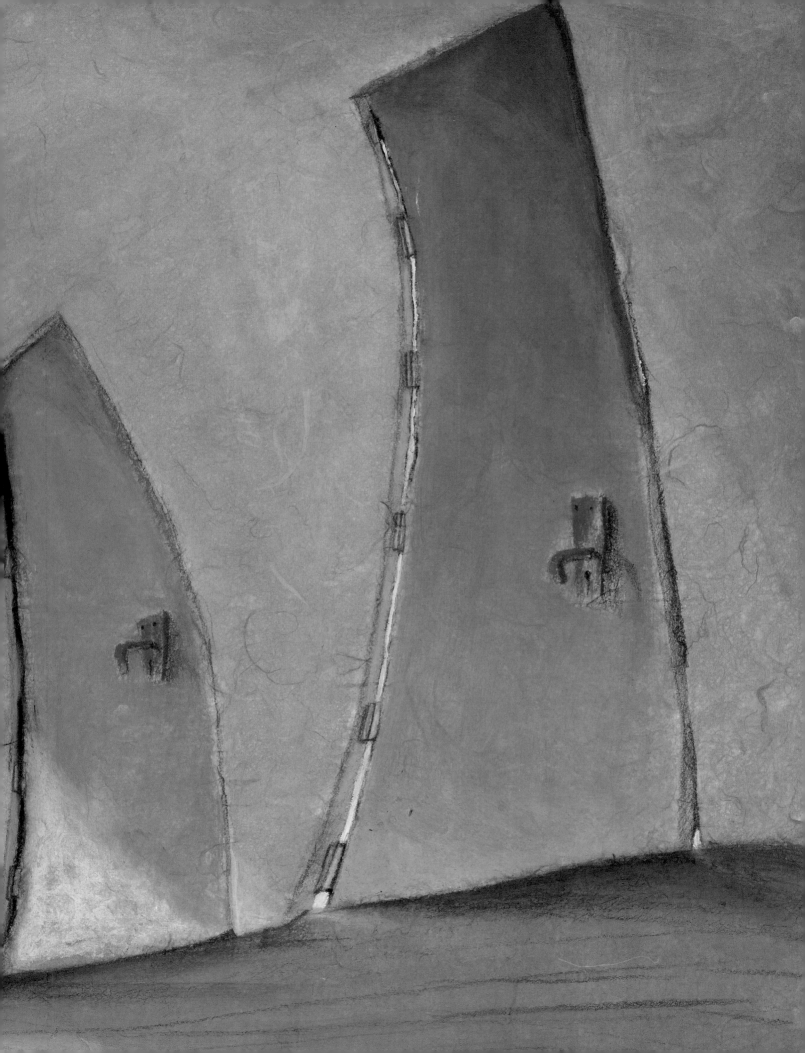

Just one door is open.
Little Tooth looks in.
There's a room full of tables.

The tables are full of ears.

At the end of the room,
there's just one free table.
It's full of books.

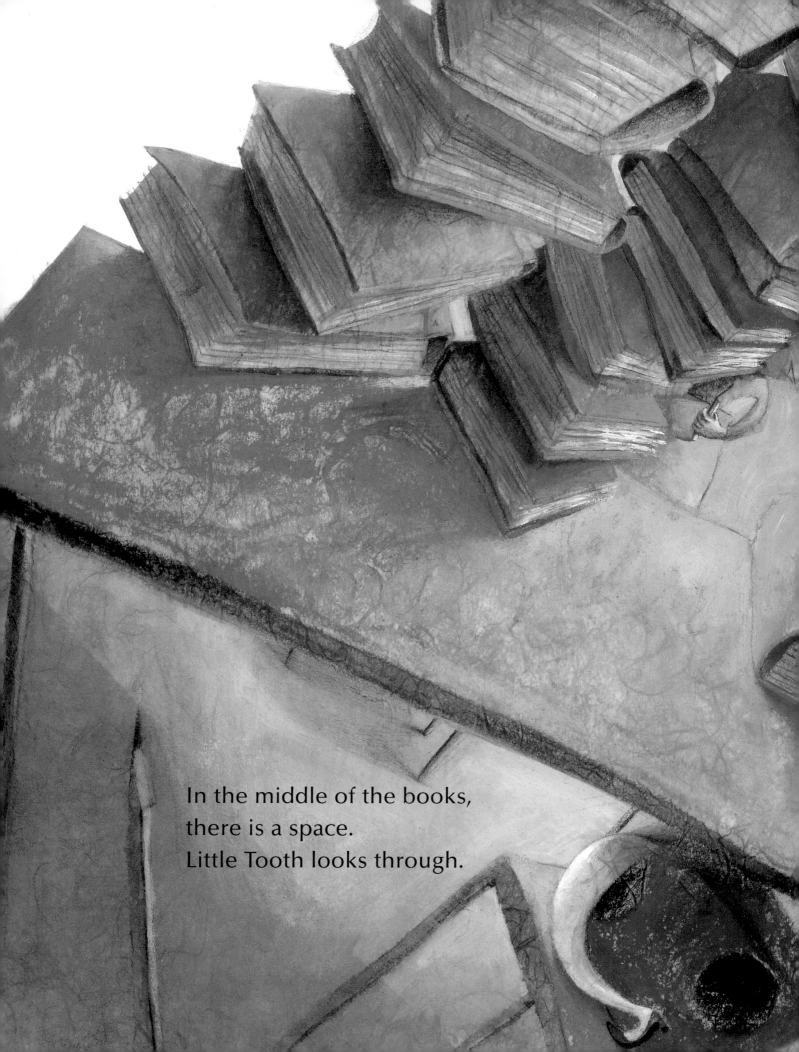

In the middle of the books,
there is a space.
Little Tooth looks through.

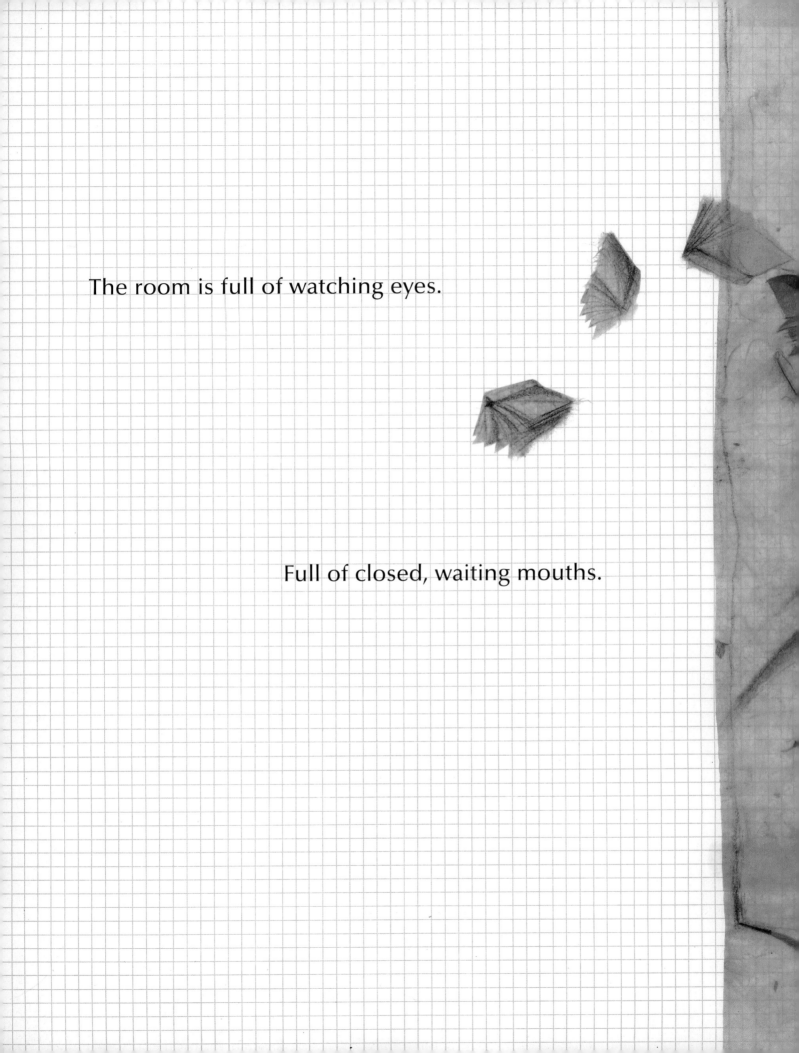

The room is full of watching eyes.

Full of closed, waiting mouths.

Behind the books, there is just one bunny.
She has her mouth open.
And she feels very afraid.

In a room very full of bags,
tables, books, ears, and bunnies,
a voice says: "I'm your teacher.
It's my first day of school as well."

Now the room
is full of smiles.